by
Polly Peters

illustrated by
Jess Stockham

Child's Play (International) Ltd
Ashworth Rd, Bridgemead, Swindon SN5 7YD UK
Swindon Auburn ME Sydney

ISBN 978-1-84643-117-3 Printed in Heshan, China
L281114CPL01151173
3 5 7 9 10 8 6 4
www.childs-play.com

What on earth can we three do?
Brother, sister, cousin too.
Just our luck! Outside, it's pouring,
Wet and windy, dull and BORING!
All our outdoor plans for play
Are ruined by the rain today.

Humpph! Sigh! Moan!
Whinge! Fuss! Groan!

All together now, one, two, three,
We've decided what we'll be:
EXPLORERS!
That's the game we'll play,
We'll make it up along the way.

Laugh! Clap! Ho ho!
Chuckle! Cheer! Let's go!

First we'll need a sturdy boat
With mast and sail - and off we'll float!
A special hat, a telescope,
A trusty dog and a length of rope.

All together now, one, two, three,
We're explorers: off to sea!
We've got provisions. We're all set.
We've even found a fishing net!

With ancient map
And spade in hand
For finding treasure
When we land,
We all jump in
And sail along,
Three explorers,
Bold and strong!

Hooray! Yell with glee!
Hurrah! Shout Yippee!

yippee
hooray
hurrah
yell
S.S. bold

Before we reach the open sea,
We must drift down the estuary.
We look around for sights and views
And vital, treasure hunting clues.

Search! Watch! Seek!
Gaze! Goggle! peek!

search

watch

gaze

seek

peek

goggle

What's that there? Let's run aground,
Weigh the anchor, look around.
Yes! We spy a secret cave.
We'll squeeze in quietly, feeling brave.

All together now, one, two, three,
We're exploring...ssshhh... silently.

It's cramped in here. It's dark and small,
With hardly any room at all.
We feel around in every nook,
And find. . .a shiny coin! Look!

But suddenly, outside, we hear
A fearsome noise that's moving near...

A charging elephant! "Watch out!
Run fast! Come on! Let's go!" we shout.

All together now, one, two, three
We're escaping, speedily!

Dash!
Race!
Scurry!
Scramble!
Zoom!
Hurry!

We lead that beast a merry chase
Through trees and swamps, to find the place
We left our boat. We grab the oars,
Jump in, and head for far-off shores.

Gasp! Gulp! Huff!
Phew! Pant! Puff!

Now, on our treasure map,
it's clear
an island should be
somewhere near.
Look left. Look right.
Look up. Surprise!
Steep cliffs soar
before our eyes.

All together now, one, two, three,
We're rock climbing – carefully!

We clamber up the long, hard climb
And pause for breath from time to time.

Not far to go.
We're nearly there!
We lie and breathe
The cool, clean air.

It's growing chilly, cold and damp.
Night is falling – let's make camp!

Through the trees and straight ahead,
A clearing where we'll make our bed.
"Exploring's tiring work," we yawn,
"Goodnight. Sleep tight until the dawn."

Snore... Snuffle... Snooze.
Doze... Sigh... Zzzzzz...

snooze
snuffle
snore
doze
Keep Out
Zzzzzz
sigh

Morning! It's a brand new day.
Let's be up and on our way.
But first, there's something that we need:
A set of wheels to put on speed.

A truck's the only way to travel
Over stones and bumpy gravel.

All together now, one, two, three,
We're exploring – lumpily.

Bash! Boing! Bump!
Crash! Tinkle! Thump!

We've driven miles, but up ahead
We'll have to go on foot instead.

Undergrowth and thorny bramble
Tangle round us as we scramble.

All together now, one, two, three.
We're exploring - scratchily.

Phew! After that we need a drink.
Where to find one? Stop and think.
What's behind this rocky wall?
What luck! A tumbling waterfall.

Slurp! Slop! Slosh!
Spill! Splash! Splosh!

A perfect pool for swimming too,
With dreamy depths of deepest blue.

All together now, one, two, three,
We're exploring - splashily.

Finally, we're getting near.
Our map says 'X marks treasure here'.
A secret cavern lies due West
And in it sits a secret chest!

slip

creep

But this is on
forbidden ground.
Step carefully,
don't make a sound.

squeak

creak

crawl

slither

Gently lift and open wide -
But that's not treasure there inside!
We yelp and squeal! We shriek and shout,
As twenty hissing snakes jump out!

Quick! We need a change of plan
To take us back where we began.
trot
whizz
vroom
zoom
This way, that way, moving fast
We set our sail for home at last.
Trot! Whizz! Vroom!
Paddle! Splash! Zoom!
splash
paddle

Land ahoy! We're nearly there.
Mmmm! Yummy smells drift on the air.
And what's that funny sound of rumbling?
Tired explorers' tummies grumbling.
All together now, one, two, three,
Exploring's hungry work, you see.

Exhausted now, on hands and knees
We track those tempting smells with ease.
Hooray! The door is open wide,
And we spy . . . Treasure, there inside!

huff

pout

sulk

We'll creep along and in we'll burst...
"No way!" says Dad. "You'll tidy first!"

Sulk! Huff! Pout! No way out!

Come on then, quickly, no delay,
We'll clear it up, put things away,
Zoom halfway round the world, like that...
And do it in three minutes flat!

Crunch! Scrunch! Crash!
Clank! Rattle! Bash!

NOW we're ready, time to munch
Our glorious explorer's lunch!
From South to North and West to East
There is no better treasure feast!

Mmmm! Hmmmm! Munch!
Yum! Slurp! Crunch!